This book belongs to

. . . .

ISBN 978-1-338-03280-2

10 9 8 7 6 5 4 3 2 1   16 17 18 19 20

Printed in China   62

First printing 2016
www.peppapig.com
Book design by Angela Jun and Becky James

Playtime for Peppa and George

Adapted by Meredith Rusu

SCHOLASTIC INC.

This is Peppa and George. Peppa is George's big sister. They share a bedroom and lots and lots of toys. Peppa and George love being brother and sister. They play fun games together every day!

One day, Peppa and George are with Mummy and Daddy Pig in the living room. Mummy Pig has to work on her computer and Daddy Pig wants to work in the garden.

"Peppa, George, why don't you two play a game?" asks Daddy Pig.

"Oh, goodie!" says Peppa. "George and I love to play games!"

"Snort, snort!" George likes that idea, too.

It is a lovely sunny day, so Peppa and George run outside.
"George, let's jump up and down in muddy puddles!"
shouts Peppa.

Splish
Splash!

But George does not want to jump in muddy puddles
today. He would like to play a different game.

"Okay," says Peppa. "We can play catch instead."

Peppa tosses a ball to George. But George does not want to play catch, either.

"George, what *would* you like to play?" asks Peppa.

"Oink, oink!" George has an idea for a new game.

Peppa follows George to Mummy and Daddy Pig's bedroom.

"There's nothing fun to play in here," says Peppa.
George shows Peppa a box at the end of the bed.
"What's this?" asks Peppa.

"Wow!" says Peppa. "George, do you want to dress up and pretend to be Mummy and Daddy?"
"Oink, oink!" George does want to dress up!

"Good idea!" says Peppa. "I want to play that game, too!"
Peppa helps George put on Daddy Pig's black hat, coat, and shoes.

"Now, you must pretend to be *exactly* like Daddy Pig," she says.

George thinks for a moment.
"SNORT!" He makes a loud noise, just like Daddy Pig.
"Very good, George!" says Peppa. "Now it's my turn."

Peppa puts on Mummy Pig's fancy dress and hat. Then she puts on the high-heeled shoes. Suddenly, Peppa is very tall. "Hee, hee, hee!" they giggle. Dressing up is very silly!

"George, what else do I need to look *exactly* like
Mummy?" Peppa asks.
"Snort, snort!" George does not know.

Peppa goes over to Mummy Pig's dresser. Sometimes Peppa watches Mummy Pig sit in front of the mirror and get ready to go out with Daddy Pig.

"I need makeup, of course!" she says.

"First, some powder." Peppa pats the pink powder on her cheeks.
Puff, puff, puff!
"Lovely!"

"Now for some lipstick."

Peppa draws on a smile using Mummy's shiny red lipstick. "How do I look?"

"SNORT!" George thinks Peppa makes a very pretty Mummy Pig.

"Come along, Daddy Pig," says Peppa. "It's time to go to work."
Peppa and George walk downstairs.

They find the real Mummy Pig working on her computer.
"Hello, Peppa. Hello, George," says Mummy Pig.
"I beg your pardon," says Peppa. "I'm not Peppa. I'm
Mummy Pig. And this is Daddy Pig."

"Oh, I see," says Mummy Pig. "Hello, Mummy Pig. Hello, Daddy Pig."

"George," Peppa whispers. "Remember to act *exactly* like Daddy."

"SNORT!" says George.

"Excuse me," says Peppa. "I have a *lot* of work to do."

She picks up Mummy Pig's telephone. "Hello. Yes! Do this, do that. Thank you!"

Then Peppa taps on the computer keyboard.
Tap! Tap! Tap!
Peppa is very good at pretending to be Mummy Pig.

alpc jfdslkjs da
a.kjdnkjasd vjsl
nnvlam nrdl
sjljdg

kas dplk jlbd

"All right. Good-bye!" she says, hanging up the phone.
"And, done! Come on, Daddy Pig. It's time you did some
work, too."

Peppa and George go back outside. They
find Daddy Pig digging a hole in the garden.
"Hello, Peppa and George," says Daddy Pig.
"I'm not Peppa. I'm Mummy Pig. And this is
Daddy Pig," says Peppa.

"Oh, I see," says Daddy Pig. "What are you up to today?"
"We are here to do some work," declares Peppa.
George jumps into the hole and begins to dig.
He is having fun pretending to work like Daddy Pig.

Peppa jumps into the hole to help George dig.
Suddenly, they hear Mummy Pig calling from the house.
"Peppa! George!"

Mummy Pig has brought ice cream for everyone.
"You must take off those muddy clothes before you eat,
Peppa and George," she says.
"Snort! I'm *Mummy Pig* and this is *Daddy Pig!*" Peppa
insists.

"Are you sure?" asks Mummy Pig. "That's a shame, because I have Peppa and George's favorite ice cream flavors. But if we can't find them . . ."

Peppa and George quickly take off the muddy clothes. "Here we are!" shouts Peppa. "We were only pretending to be you and Daddy Pig."

"Ho, ho! You really had us fooled," says Daddy Pig.
"It was George's idea to dress up," says Peppa.
"Oink!" George nods, licking his ice cream.
"You both did a very good job," says Mummy Pig.

Peppa and George love ice cream.
And they love pretending to be Mummy and Daddy Pig.
But most of all, they love being brother and sister.